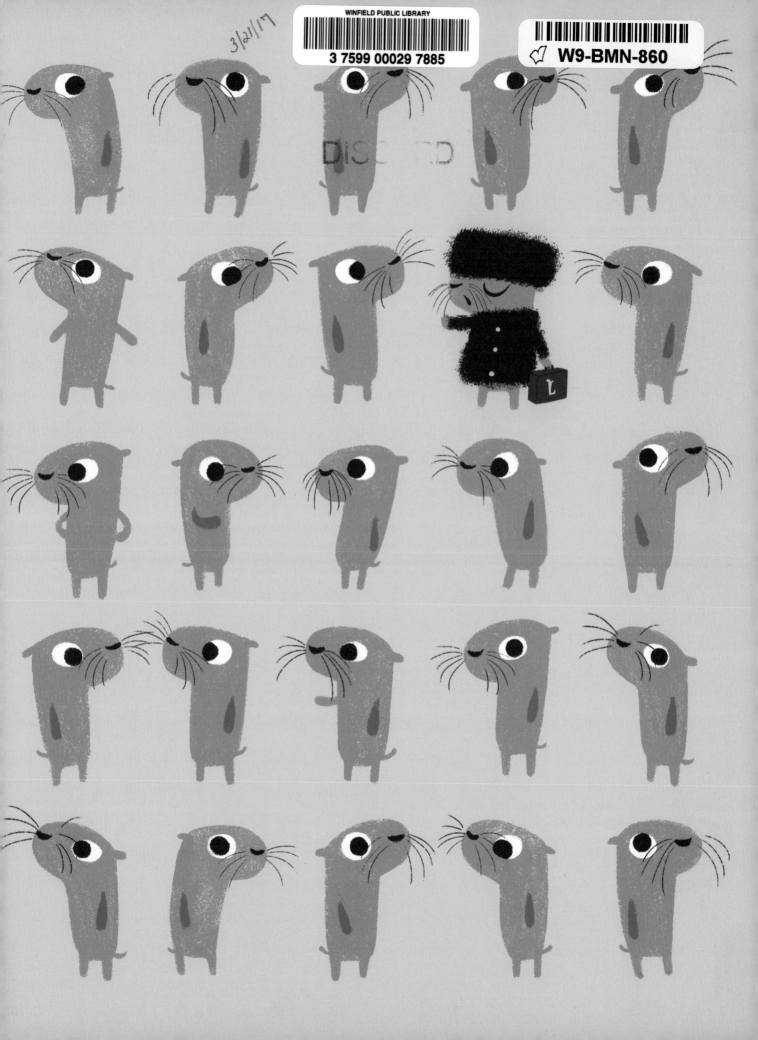

WINFIELD PUBLIC LIBRARY

3 7599 00029 7885

W9-BMN-860

3/21/17

To Johnny K, Hailey, and Josephine. —J. B.

For Leo. —N. S.

STERLING CHILDREN'S BOOKS
New York

An Imprint of Sterling Publishing Co., Inc.
1166 Avenue of the Americas
New York, NY 10036

STERLING CHILDREN'S BOOKS and the distinctive Sterling Children's Books logo
are trademarks of Sterling Publishing Co., Inc.

Text © 2016 by John Briggs
Illustrations © 2016 by Nicola Slater

All rights reserved. No part of this publication may be reproduced, stored in a retrieval system,
or transmitted in any form or by any means (including electronic, mechanical, photocopying,
recording, or otherwise) without prior written permission from the publisher.

ISBN 978-1-4549-1819-6

Distributed in Canada by Sterling Publishing Co., Inc
c/o Canadian Manda Group, 664 Annette Street
Toronto, Ontario, Canada M6S 2C8
Distributed in the United Kingdom by GMC Distribution Services
Castle Place, 166 High Street, Lewes, East Sussex, England BN7 1XU
Distributed in Australia by Capricorn Link (Australia) Pty. Ltd.
P.O. Box 704, Windsor, NSW 2756, Australia

For information about custom editions, special sales, and premium and corporate purchases,
please contact Sterling Special Sales at 800-805-5489 or specialsales@sterlingpublishing.com.

Manufactured in China
Lot #:
2 4 6 8 10 9 7 5 3 1
06/16

www.sterlingpublishing.com

The artwork for this book was created digitally
Art directed and designed by Merideth Harte

LEAPING LEMMINGS!

by
JOHN BRIGGS

illustrated by
NICOLA SLATER

STERLING CHILDREN'S BOOKS
New York

Can you tell these two lemmings apart?

No?

That's because all lemmings look alike, sound alike, and act alike.

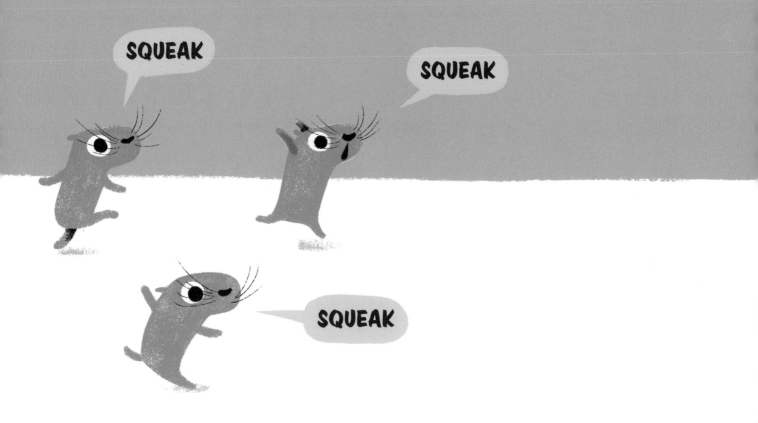

When all the other lemmings dug tunnels to keep warm, he went sledding with the puffins.

Winfield Public Library

When the other lemmings squeaked and squealed, he banged on the bongos he got from the seals.

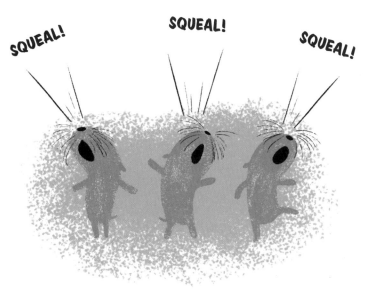

When the other lemmings ate moss from under a rock, he ordered pepperoni pizza with extra cheese and hot sauce.

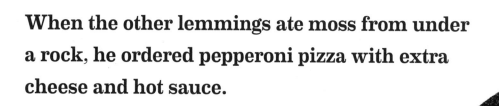

Hey guys, look— it melts snow!

Yes, this lemming was an odd duck.
He stood out in every lemming photo.

Norway trip

And he was easy to spot at hide-and-seek.

The other lemmings tried to talk with him.

"He wants to be called Larry."

"I'm not calling him Larry."

"What's a Larry?"

"No lemming's ever been called Larry."

"No lemming's ever been called anything."

"I hear he wants to be called Mary."

The lemmings called a big meeting,
and they only had one question:

Larry knew he didn't fit in, so he tried something else no other lemming had ever done.

Winfield Public Library

He went to live with the seals.

He moved in with the puffins.

You live on CLIFFS?!

He visited the polar bears.

Larry ran all the way home to the lemmings, who were also running—straight for the cliff!

Larry raced in front of his friends as fast
as he could. He made a sharp U-turn . . .
and the lemmings followed him!

And the lemmings didn't stop following Larry until every last one was safe at home enjoying a hero's feast of pepperoni pizza with extra cheese and hot sauce.

LARRY

"If all your friends jumped off a cliff, would you?"

Larry smiled to see his friends thinking for themselves.